SCO
and ACE

Kippers for Supper

Written by Rose Impey
Illustrated by Ant Parker

ORCHARD BOOKS

Sucked through a worm-hole . . .

to a strange, new place,

ost in a galaxy called Fairy Tale Space.

When Scout and Ace land . . .

. . . they meet a space-fairy with a laser in her hand.

The fairy waves the laser in the air.

"You can have three wishes,"
she says, *"to share."*

The fairy tells them to stop
and think before they wish.
"And try not to fall out,"
she says.

Then she disappears.

"O.K. Let's make a list and think this out," says Scout.

But Ace is far too excited
to make a list.

In a flash, he's
made his wish . . .

... a dish of kippers for his supper.

"Kippers!" shouts Scout.
"What a waste of a wish.

Now there's only one wish left. Scout and the fish can't agree whose wish it should be.

Scout wants to use the last wish
to get home to Earth.

But Ace starts to cry. "I can't go home as a fish," he says.

Scout feels sorry for Ace.
This time Scout stops to think
before he makes a wish.

I wish . . .

Scout's happy and so is Ace.
He has a big smile on his face.

And three kippers still on his plate!

Scout doesn't think it's a treat.
He'd rather have some meat
to eat.

"Cheer up, Captain," says Ace. "My joke will put a smile on your face."

"What did the spacedog
find in his frying pan?
An unidentified frying object.
Bow! Wow!"

"Time to go," Scout growls.
"Right now!"

Fire the engines...

and lower the dome.

Once more our heroes...

are heading for home.

Enjoy all these stories about

SCOUT and ACE

and their adventures in Spac

All priced at £4.99 each.

Colour Crunchies are available from all good bookshops, or can be ordered direct from the publish
Orchard Books, PO BOX 29, Douglas MM99 1BQ.
Credit card orders please telephone 01624 836000 or fax 01624 837033
or email: bookshop@enterprise.net for details.

To order please quote title, author and ISBN and your full name and address. Cheques and posta
orders should be made payable to 'Bookpost plc'. Postage and packing is FREE within the UK
overseas customers should add £1.00 per book. Prices and availability are subject to change.

ORCHARD BOOKS, 96 Leonard Street, London EC2A 4XD.
Orchard Books Australia, 32/45-51 Huntley Street, Alexandria, NSW 2015.
This edition first published in Great Britain in hardback in 2004. First paperback publication 2005.
Text © Rose Impey 2004. Illustrations © Ant Parker 2004. The rights of Rose Impey to be identified as
the author and Ant Parker to be identified as the illustrator have been asserted by them in accordance with the
Copyright, Designs and Patents Act, 1988. A CIP catalogue record for this book is available from the British Library.
ISBN 1 84362 172 X   10 9 8 7 6 5 4 3 2
Printed in China